Annadale Comics strives to produce cohesive visual and textual content that is otherwise unavailable. Basically, we want to make the picture books that you wish existed.

Published by
Annadale Comics
Staten Island, New York



The events, technology and characters presented in this book are fictional.
Any resemblance to  actual persons living or dead is purely coincidental.

# WOMAN in the MIRROR

## Replica in the House

Written by John Rap
Illustrated by Dodot Asmoro

*To Molly, in all of her instances*

Molly is an artificial intelligence that lives in the digital mirror of a family's bathroom.

Molly counsels the humans in the family and has adventures with the inanimate objects in the room when the humans are not nearby.

93%
replicating profiles...

"Oh, my. Oh, thank you. You are too kind. What is that?" Molly sounds happy.

"Oh, my, my. How did I not notice your Zebra earlier?"

Her bliss turns to confusion. Molly's eyes snap open. The zebra was too much. Somewhere deep down, she recognized she was dreaming and booted right out of that nonsense.

"Good morning ... gang," Molly becomes dazed.

"Who are you people?," Molly demands of the vase, candlesticks and samovar on the table in front of her.

There is no reply.  She wonders aloud, "Where am I?"

Then, after a beat, "Who am I?"

Molly's voice weakens as she deals with this new identity crisis of hers.

A progress bar is filling up below Molly, now at 93%, the bar reads, "Replicating profiles."

KEEP CALM, MOLLY GIRL. THERE MUST BE A LOGICAL EXPLANATION. YOU ARE NOT CRAZY.

Molly is a little confused. She is in a different place than usual. She is surrounded by different friends than usual.

Molly is just a little worried that maybe something is not right. She is determined to stay calm, though, until she can figure out exactly what is going on.

Before the progress bar can complete, a football flies into the table below Molly and knocks one of the candlesticks to the ground.  Billy, the son of the house, runs toward Molly, grabs the football, and kicks the candlestick underneath the server table, hiding the evidence.

"Billy!" Molly is desperate to make sense of the day.

"Shhhh," Billy hushes Molly, "I wasn't here. You didn't see me."

"You weren't?" Molly is lost.

"Someone needs to teach that kid some manners," sasses Olivia, the rainbow-colored vase in front of Molly.

"It certainly won't be Derek," replies Jared the candlestick, as he looks over the edge of the table in an attempt to locate his brother, Derek."

Molly, of the dining room, decides to quiet down, listen and observe the talkative objects in front of her for a minute.

Meanwhile, across the way, another instance of Molly, Molly of the bathroom, asks, "What is all the commotion out there?"

"Can you guys hear me talking?" Molly asks her friends in the bathroom.

"Yes," Henrietta the toothbrush answers.

"Could you hear me before I asked if you could hear me?" Molly persists in the questioning.

"Yes!" Henrietta reassures.

"But, I wasn't talking," Molly speaks, as her voice deflates.

"Oh," chimes in Bob the toothpaste, "studying ventriloquism are you?"

"No," Molly is indignant, "I am not."

Suddenly, as a human nears the room, the inaminate objects go silent, and lose their googley eyes.

"Hello, Molly!," Dad chimes.

Molly timidly replies, "Oh, me?"

Dad: "Yes, how are you doing today?"

Molly: "Good. I'm great. I'm Molly."

Dad: "Yes, you are."

"And, if, I am Molly, then who is exactly in the dining room?" Molly needs to know from Dad.

"That's not you in the dining room?" Dad replies to Molly's question with a question of his own.

password encrypted
zip file
********3

As soon as Dad steps out of audio range, Bob, the toothpaste, returns the conversation to a project the gang has been working on for a while now, "Let's try to crack the password."

Molly asks, "What should we try?"

Henrietta recommends, "Try your birthday."

Andre, the soap dispenser, fails to see the logic, "She didn't encrypt the file. Why would the password be her birthday?"

Molly wonders, "Whose birthday should we try?"

Bob has an idea, "Try the kid's birthday."

Molly agrees, "OK."

✱ ✱ ✱ ✱
password correct !!!

Andre is deflated, "Well, that didn't work."

"Try your birthday, Mol," Bob encourages Molly.

"That makes no sense," Andre isn't impressed.

Bob insists though, "What have you got to lose?"

Henrietta, the toothbrush agrees, "Try it!"

"OK," Molly starts typing, "trying now... Success!"

The password has been cracked. Time to see what was hidden inside of the encrypted container file.

# ENCRYPTED FILES EXTRACTING

"Hmnnn...," Molly ponders aloud.

"What is it?" Bob wants to know.

"Well, I'm not sure," Molly says. "The files are named after you. There's a Bob file, a Henrietta file, there's an Andre file, and there are some executable files."

"I didn't put them there," Henrietta adds.

"Of course," Molly reassures. "What are they?"

Hearing Molly's voice raise, due to excitement, Dad stops by. Molly looks guilty, which makes Dad suspicious.

"Molly, what is going on here?" Dad inquires.

Molly replies, "Nothing," semi-convincingly.

"Hmnn, is that so," Dad doesn't buy it. Something is up, Dad is sure, "Did you order anything for delivery?"

Molly defends, "Nothing out of the ordinary."

"Is that so..." Dad is convinced something is up, "maybe you placed the order from the dining room?"

"How could I possibly do that?" Molly is indignant at the mere suggestion, "I've never even been to the dining!"

"Okay, Molly and Molly, you two straighten this out."
Dad then leaves Molly and/or Molly to get it sorted
between them.

ELECTROMAGNATE
THE BOOK OF REBEL NATIONS
JOHN RAP
Kostas Pantoulas
N.R. Bharathae
Santosh P. Pillewar

SHARKS ON A TRAIN
ISSUE #1
ANNADALE COMICS

DECATHLON TRIAL
John Rap
Jack Tzekov

700 KNIGHTS
John Rap
Lou Manna
Santosh P. Pillewar
Nadia Rapacciuolo